THE MANHOOD MANUAL

A Comic Adventure

Steve Stanaszak

Illustrated by
Steve Stanaszak and Jamie Ludovise

Library of Congress Control Number: 2016917221

CreateSpace Independent Publishing Platform,
North Charleston, SC

ISBN-10: 1537175653
ISBN-13: 978-1537175652

This book is typeset in Sketchnote Text
and Sketchnote Square
Copyright © Delve Fonts

To Michael and Megan

Life doesn't need to be perfect to be wonderful.

MANHOOD

A man's usefulness depends upon his living up to his ideals insofar as he can.

It is hard to fail, but it is worse never to have tried to succeed.

All daring and courage, all iron endurance of misfortune-make for a finer, nobler type of manhood.

Only those are fit to live who do not fear to die and none are fit to die who have shrunk from the joy of life and the duty of life.

Theodore Roosevelt

Hello there. I am a man. Are you curious

about how I became a man? If you are, turn the

page and keep reading . . .

After thirteen
long years, I've
made it. I'm a
man! Seriously.
When my parents
introduce me to

anyone these days in our little town of Horn Hill,
they always say, "This is Mr. Jeffrey Crandle,
our fine young man." Ask my little brother Ben
and he'll tell you the same thing. There is no

reason to doubt
it — I'M A MAN!
As a man,
I'm thankful for
what I can call

not a bribe

Ben

mine. For starters, I am *very* thankful for my own bedroom — with a lock. My best friend P.J. doesn't have a lock on his bedroom door and he is terrorized daily by his parents. Even worse, P.J. shares a bedroom with his little brother. I'm not sure which would be more annoying. Would it be worse to be subjected to surprise inspections of your unlocked room without even the chance to wipe your tracks? Or, would it be more offensive to have some other creature in your room watching you all of the time? I guess both are slightly better than sharing a room with your sister, but not by much.

Anyway, in my bedroom I have many of the things that make me the man I am. I keep stuff like my award-winning pinewood derby car and my bobble head collection on display for everyone

to see. I hide

other things for

one reason or

another. I stash

my wallet in my

sock drawer because my older sister Kate has

sticky hands. She claims she just borrows my

money, but we both know she is stealing it. I also

have a little container I call Fort Box. If you

remove the bottom drawer of my desk, it just so

happens that Fort

Box slides nicely

underneath. I keep

my treasured items

Fort Box

in Fort Box and right now it holds the following great loot:

1. A guarantee certificate from an old fishing pole

2. A couple of packets of ketchup

3. A Hal's Hardware Store honorary name badge

4. A half-empty can of Famous Ivan's Itching Powder

5. A photo of my bulldog Charlie dressed up for Halloween

6. My dad's slightly charred Major Matt Mason action figure

7. A roll of dimes

Last but not least, I have a couple of candy bars in Fort Box just in case I'm sent to my room for a lengthy period of time. (Yes, it has happened.)

I stockpile other manly things under my

bed. Not to get

off track here,

but there is a

surprising

amount of

storage space under a bed and no one in my

family uses the space as well

as I do. When I just can't get

my dirty clothes to the

laundry chute because I'm too

tired — under the bed. When I

don't feel like doing homework

that might gobble up valuable

time better spent playing with

Kate (Ugh!)

friends — under the bed. You get the idea. Sooner or later, someone is going to look under there and it will not be a pretty sight. I now have thirteen years of stuff neatly organized under my bed.

So, yeah, if you haven't figured it out yet, I know what I'm doing. *I'm a man!* Dad swears that everything you need to know about becoming a man comes to our door once a week in the Sunday edition of the *Horn Hill Herald*. Dad happens to be the Editor-in-Chief of the *Herald* so you really wouldn't expect anything else, right? Sure, I enjoy the Sunday comics and even the Trophy Tales section where they put the pictures of men with their big fishing catches. But I've never read *anything* in the *Herald* that was the key to *my* manhood.

I often think back to all of the times I've gotten into trouble because I didn't have someone to show me the ropes. There have been so many cool ideas that have turned into big problems for me over the years. I've decided to dedicate myself to guiding others so that they can benefit from my mistakes. How can I help you? Well, let me tell you.

My dad reads these books about

how to get rich. My mom reads a lot of books with shirtless, long-haired men on the cover, but she sometimes reads books about how to cook better too. (Those books are gifts from my dad but he tells her they're from us kids.) Even my sister is in on the self-help book craze, believe it or not. Although it isn't going to help, Kate reads books about how to make boys like her. (Yeah, right!) But I haven't found *one* book out there that helped me become the man I am. It was just pure hard work. The way I see it, my bumps and bruises are your express ticket to manhood.

So, for all you boys out there, this is *The Manhood Manual*. It is the one and only super self-help handbook that will show you how to be just like me — a successful, well-adjusted, good looking thirteen-year-old man! If you're ready, let's go on my comic adventure and get you to the other side.

MY FIRST CATCH

The Cool Idea

I remember the sunny Saturday morning

like it was yesterday. With a slight breeze and

nothing but blue skies, it just smelled like summer.

Normally, if I didn't escape fast enough, a day like

this was filled with nonstop forced labor — aka

yard work — pulling around sticks and other

crap in an old red wagon with nothing but bad memories attached to it.

But this Saturday was different. Dad and I were heading to Croaker Pond to fish for a monster with my new Stryker XPX 2000 rod and reel. This was no ordinary rod and reel, mind you. The Stryker XPX 2000 was a super-sensitive fish magnet given to me by my dad on my tenth birthday. According to the ad in the *Herald*, when the red light on the pole is flashing, the Stryker XPX 2000 emits a special sound (patent pending) only heard by big fish. Not surprisingly, the Stryker is guaranteed to catch *monster* fish.

With the guarantee of the catch of a lifetime spoiling our sleep, Dad and I woke up early and packed our gear. As usual, I finished

packing

much

sooner

than Dad.

Based on

the gear

we assembled (including the Stryker XPX 2000,

of course), I was patiently buying what he was

selling.

Um, we're only going for the day, right Dad?!?

As with all fishing trips with Dad, I was reminded that the key to a good day on the pond would boil down to the Fishing Fundamentals. My dad is a "list guy," so he actually has the list typed on a well-worn piece of paper in our tackle box.

According to Dad, Grandpa added Fishing Fundamental number four when Dad was a kid because Dad

Fishing Fundamentals

1. The right pole.
2. The right bait.
3. The right spot.
4. Patience.

couldn't sit still on one trip and ended up falling out of the boat. Dad says he learned to take fishing seriously after that mishap. I listened to Dad's motivational speech and promised him I would follow the Fishing Fundamentals on our trip.

When we arrived at Croaker Pond, we weren't the only anglers looking for a shot at the big one. After checking out the competition to make sure no one else was working with the Stryker XPX 2000, we set up our position near a large tree providing shade over the water — a perfect place for a monster to hide on a sunny day. We had the right pole, the right bait and now, the right spot. All we needed was some patience.

The Big Problem

A beautiful morning turned into a beautiful afternoon . . . without a *single* bite. Dad and I were unfazed. In fact, Dad

was snoozing most of the afternoon with his pole held snuggly in his hands. Based on the constant activity of the other anglers, we knew the fish were biting. They had to head our way eventually.

After checking to make sure the Stryker XPX 2000 was still activated, I leaned my pole on a "No Swimming" sign and walked along the shore looking for signs of life. Just then, it happened. I got a bite.

Unfortunately, the nibble on the Stryker XPX 2000 quickly turned into a yank as the pole slid off the sign. I shot across the rocky shore and the Stryker skipped along in front of me, out of reach. Finally, I dove for the pole and grasped the handle. I tried to hold on, but right when I thought I had it secured, a giant fish leapt out of the water and, in an instant, dove back in. It seemed to happen in slow motion and it appeared this monster was smiling at me. The pole came

whipping out of my hands and into the deep dark water of the pond. The Stryker XPX 2000 was gone and I was swimming in the pond!

Dad jumped up from his nap and pulled me out of the water. We gawked at each other, trying to understand what had happened. Without talking at all, Dad dug out the first aid kit. A few bandages later we both exclaimed, "NOW THAT WAS A MONSTER FISH!"

Out of the corner of my eye, I saw Dad's pole quiver. We had another bite. Could this be the same monster? Dad grabbed his pole and handed it to me. With newfound strength, I began the fight. I struggled to bring this monster to the shore. As I fought the as-yet-unseen menace, I knew this must be the beast that had stolen my Stryker XPX 2000. After fighting for several minutes, I finally landed him.

But this wasn't the same beast. In fact, I was surprised this little guy was able to get himself on the hook.

Even though the fish wasn't a keeper, my dad took out the camera and asked a woman walking by to take our photo. The embarrassing photo is framed and hanging in the den next to

Dad's membership certificate in the Clean Rivers and Ponds Society. My Dad is smiling ear-to-ear. And me, well, although I'm a little beat up in the picture, I'm sort of smiling too. Dad submitted the picture to the *Herald* and they printed it the following week in Trophy Tales. A complete embarrassment!

The Lesson Learned

Dad and I showed the rest of the family the picture of our catch at dinner. But the *big* story was the monster that got away with my Stryker XPX 2000. Mom and Kate snickered and kept asking us what *really* happened at the pond. Dad and I knew that this was a day we would never forget. We hooked the biggest fish in Croaker Pond and we intended to go back and somehow land it (and my Stryker XPX 2000) again. The next morning we read the *Herald* (well, I read the comics at least) and planned how we would capture this beast. We have not caught him yet, but we will.

So I've started out with a pretty easy lesson for you: Even if you have all the right stuff on your list, even if *all* the fundamentals are in place, sometimes things don't go as planned. So be a man. Take your lumps and keep smiling — even when a monster steals your Stryker XPX 2000!

Fishing Fundamentals

1. The right pole.
2. The right bait.
3. The right spot.
4. Patience.
5. WATCH YOUR POLE!!!

Now that you've got the hang of it, let's move on to a tastier lesson.

A KETCHUP KAPER

The Cool Idea

I love ketchup! Then again, who doesn't? For me, ketchup is a key part of most meals because it goes with *everything*. But no one else in my family feels the way I do about ketchup.

My mom is a great cook. She is also a nurse at Horn Hill Hospital. You'd think a nurse who works with blood and guts all day would appreciate delicious red ketchup, but that's not the case. She just doesn't seem to get ketchup.

Ketchup has saved me from some of the most disgusting meals you can imagine. Let's say Mom's working late and Dad makes some gross dinner that even my dog Charlie won't touch.

What do you do as a man? Throw some ketchup on it and toss it down the old food chute!

I've seen ketchup containers in all shapes and sizes. My favorite is the traditional tiny packet that you can shove in your pocket to take with you -- just in case you run into a nasty food emergency away from home. As a man, the ketchup packet is a

basic item that must be carried with you at all times. Mom always tells me it is just one of many condiments and gives me a funny look whenever I stuff ketchup packets in my pockets before heading out for the day. I still don't know what the word "condiment" means, but ketchup is definitely a cool one.

The Big Problem

But what about that little packet? What keeps the ketchup inside? Why doesn't the ketchup ever leak

out? This mystery baffled me until one fateful day, during a very boring car ride with Mom and Ben. Like almost any thought that entered my head when I was a boy, the magical source of the ketchup packet's sturdiness consumed me. I was determined to get to the bottom of it.

Poke, squeeze, bend and twist — how does the ketchup stay put? What is keeping it in the

packet? What is the packet made of — some

super strong indestructible plastic from outer

space?

What if I poke, squeeze, bend and twist a

little harder? Nope, nothing. I can't even smell

ketchup. Why not?

What if I poke, squeeze, bend, twist and

squeeze even harder . . . .

Turns out the little ketchup packet can in fact explode if you squeeze it just right. And despite its small size, the packet holds quite a bit of ketchup! The much bigger problem is that to a mother and nurse, ketchup sprayed all over her son in the back seat of a car apparently looks a lot like blood.

Thinking I was dying or something, Mom

slammed on the brakes. I tried to brace myself,

but Mom really knows how to hit the brakes.

Tragically, this caused the ketchup to get mashed

onto the seats and just about everywhere else.

(A delicious mess, right?) The even bigger problem

was that Mom's fear that I hurt myself quickly

turned to an anger like nothing I had ever seen. I

think this had a lot to do with the fact that the

unmistakable smell of yummy ketchup had made its way to the front seat. Oops!

The Lesson Learned

Because manhood lessons can be tough to grasp, I've started out with a couple of easy ones. There are four big manhood lessons in this tragic car ride, so let's see how many you figured out. First, the ketchup packet is NOT made of indestructible plastic from outer space. Second, moms do not like surprises while driving. Third, moms can switch from worried to angry faster than greased lightning. Finally, the *big* manhood lesson learned is that the back seat of a car is not the best place to conduct experiments, no matter how bored you are.

The smell of ketchup in my Mom's car for
the next several years was comforting to me at
first. But Mom always seemed to get a little
upset on the warm days when you could really
make out the musty ketchup smell. She mumbled
under her breath, her face pinched, and I could
make out my name and something about a
military academy. All things considered, I will miss
the pleasant smell, but I was happy when my
parents traded in Mom's car for a new, ketchup-

free car. And Mom even picked my favorite color.
.. RED!

But let's get serious. Becoming a man isn't just about fishing tales and ketchup packets. No, becoming a man is hard work.

YOU'RE HIRED!

The Cool Idea

Let's face it, one of the tough parts of
becoming a man is the Chore Chart. You know,
that goofy list of jobs
that jolts you from a
carefree kid to a
contributing family
member. And like a
father's failed
motivational speech,

Chore Charts come in many shapes and sizes.
Some look like colorful posters suitable for
framing. Some are set up like games. The latest
Chore Chart rage is to turn them into mobile

phone apps so kids can brag about the chores they do every week. REALLY?!? Parents can be downright twisted. Whether you're talking smiley-face stickers or the highly overrated gold star, the Chore Chart is nothing more than dressed-up, crappy

W - O - R - K.

For $7.50 each week, my chores are a grind. My "list guy" Dad types up our chores and posts them on the refrigerator every Sunday.

JEFFREY'S CHORE CHART

1. The Basics: Clean up bedroom daily
2. Daily Teamwork: Feed Charlie and take him for a walk with Ben
3. Morning "Feel Good" Job: Make bed
4. Daily Sister Bonding: Set and clear dinner table with Kate
5. Weekly Grossness: Empty garbage cans
6. Skill Booster Challenge: Change burnt out light bulbs
7. Weekly Brain Trainer: Do homework
8. MYSTERY CHORE! Who wants to earn some more money!?!

As you can see, Dad tries to make it fun, but it isn't. The jobs don't change much either. Sometimes I'm walking Charlie with Ben and sometimes with Kate. In the summer I mow the lawn and in the winter I shovel snow. The Skill Booster Challenge is always something Mom has asked Dad to do; instead, he uses the Chore Chart to get me to do it! I can earn anywhere from an extra $1.00 up to $5.00 if I agree to do the Mystery Chore for the week. The catch is that I don't know what the Mystery Chore is or how much cash is at play ahead of time. I fell for this once. Dad made me scrub the toilets for a buck. Never again! About the only good that has ever come from the Chore Chart is the twenty dollar bill I found while vacuuming the couch. I think it fell out of Kate's pocket when she fell

asleep on the couch — which is where the phrase

"you snooze, you lose" comes from I guess.

On Ben's seventh birthday, he became

Chore Chart eligible and earned the exact same

amount as me. This is completely unfair for one

simple reason: Ben's list is stupid!! Here is a look

at Ben's cupcake Chore Chart for last week:

1. The Basics: Give Mom and Dad a BIG hug!
2. Teamwork: Take Charlie for a walk with Jeffrey
3. Morning "Feel Good" Job: Brush your teeth
4. Daily Sister Bonding: Draw a picture with Kate
5. Weekly Grossness: Watch Jeffrey empty garbage
6. Mystery Chore! Who wants some more money?!?

BIG BEN!

Good Job!

Because he is a dork, Ben always says yes to the Mystery Chore. Ben's last big Mystery Chore was to say "thank you" to Mom after dinner for a week. Despite my protests for new chores and more money, the Chore Charts did not change. So I decided to try something new.

In order to get a job as a man, you need to fill out an application and get hired. The Chore

Chart turns this idea on its head because you're hired for a job you never applied for and never wanted. I decided that I should be able to interview for the jobs on my Chore Chart. After some serious talks, Dad agreed with my brilliant idea.

The Big Problem

Dad explained that "the devil is in the details" and insisted on some ground rules. First, I would need to respond to a formal job ad — like one in the *Herald*. So he made one up.

LATEST JOBS!

HELP WANTED

Do you like to play new video games?

Well, then you need a job!

Make BIG $$$ by doing chores that you help pick!!

For interview call 242-222-1010

DON'T DELAY!

MUST HAVE GOOD REFERENCES!

ALL DECISIONS FINAL!

$$$$$$$$$$$$$

NEED A CHANGE?

Second, Dad required me to interview for the job. Third, Dad stressed that this was an agreement between the two of us and nobody else, so I needed to accept the decisions made in the hiring process. With thoughts of my sweet new chores and big

bankroll in my head, I eagerly agreed. I came to the interview in my suit. After making a great-looking first impression, I pulled out my sweet resume laying out my skills and providing a slam-dunk celebrity reference — Mom!

As expected, Dad took detailed notes during the interview. I offered friendly compliments and followed this up with great examples of what I could do to help him every day. At the end of the interview, I urged him to speak with my reference. I told Dad that my reference knows me better than I know myself. For dramatic effect, Dad mailed me a letter with his hiring decision:

The Crandle Family
4565 Bruce Lane
Horn Hill, USA

Re: Job

Dear Mr. Jeffrey Crandle:

Thank you for interviewing with me. I am very impressed with you. After speaking with your reference, I am convinced that you are the perfect candidate for a new Chore Chart. Your reference spoke very highly of you and agreed that she knows you better than you know yourself. She believes you need new and challenging chores.

I am pleased to inform you that you're hired! Your old Chore Chart is gone and the new one comes with a raise to $9.50 per week. It includes all of your old jobs, plus you can choose a NEW one from one of these two great chores:

1. Clean the toilets once a week
2. Watch Ben once a week while Mom is shopping

As noted in the ad, **ALL DECISIONS ARE FINAL!**

Thank you.

Dad

Mr. Charles R. Crandle (aka "Dad")

The Lesson Learned

What!?! What just happened? I demanded more money and to pick my chores. I received more money and I guess, um, I'm picking my chores. But what went wrong?!? Well, for starters, I don't think I'll use my Mom as a reference when I look for a real job. I did, however, get what I asked for in the end. Did I learn a lesson? Sure. Be careful what you ask for from your dad because the small stuff matters. Dad has some weird sayings, but I now know what he means when he says, "the devil is in the details." What I learned is simple — a young man in the Crandle house is worth $9.50 a week.

And you know what? That's more than Ben gets

for his cupcake chores!

MANHOLES

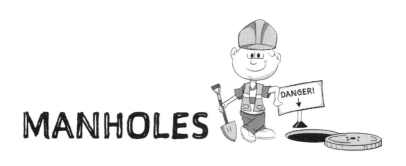

BUSTED!

While we are on the topic of the small stuff,

let's take a break from the big problems so I can

share with you some important tips I like to call

Manholes. You know, the holes you see in the

street?!? Let's put a lid on as many Manholes as

possible so you don't fall in one. In this

installment of Manholes, we'll take a look at

some really dumb moves. When it comes to these

manly missteps, no matter how fast you come up

with an excuse, you're BUSTED!

Much like ketchup, testing any product that emits fumes is never a good idea while waiting for your dad in his car.

Sweet talking your little brother after a fight never works if your mom can clearly see the evidence.

There will be at least one broken window on the road to manhood, and your dad will still be mad even if you claim you're practicing for the pros.

Think about ALL of the evidence before giving a statement.

There are times when slowly chewing your food helps you come up with a better story.

Avoiding the above situations altogether is the best move. But if you can't do that, just fess up, take what's coming, and then make sure you find time to unwind and release the stress of becoming a man!

GONE FISHING . . . AGAIN

Becoming a man is not easy. Let's take a break and go fishing. After the XPX 2000 incident at Croaker Pond, Dad and I would head back and try to catch the monster every chance we could. Sometimes we'd take a boat out to the middle of Croaker Pond. Follow our lines to figure out which pole has the monster fish on it!

BROTHERS 'TIL THE BOTTOM

All for one and one for all
My brother and my friend
What fun we have
The time we share
Brothers 'til the end.

The Cool Idea

I will tell you right now that my little brother Ben can be a huge pain. If he senses trouble of any sort, he immediately tells Mom and Dad. Normally, the trouble is something I'm doing! Even though he's a tattletale, I don't mind hanging out with him from time to time. One of those times was the morning Dad gave us a new red wagon. Dad claimed it was just like the one he'd used on his *Horn Hill Herald* paper route as a kid. With four wheels, a handle and a place to sit, this was the closest thing to a car Dad had ever turned over to us. The first thing that naturally came to my mind when I saw it was, "How fast can this thing go?" We waved to Dad from the driveway as he drove off to work that morning, probably congratulating himself on what two fine boys he was raising.

Fast forward about thirty-six seconds. At the end of our street is Horn Hill, the namesake of our town. It is a rather large hill. It would be

great for winter sledding except for the fact that

there is quite a bit of traffic at the bottom and

no way to stop a sled. I proposed we take the

wagon
down Horn
Hill. After
all, unlike a
sled, we
could
steer the

HORN HILL
(enlarged to suggest danger)

wagon to avoid traffic. Ben loved the idea.

Climbing up Horn Hill, I just knew I wanted to

hammer this wagon back to the bottom. At the

top, I wasn't so sure. This needed a test run and

Ben happily strapped on the football helmet and

climbed aboard. As I gave the wagon a shove back down the hill, I envisioned a future in car racing for the Crandle brothers.

The Big Problem

Wow! What a mistake!

I wonder if Horn Hill is named for the car horns that can be heard quite clearly from the top. I'm not sure, but I give Ben a lot of credit for hanging on the entire way down. Horn Hill really didn't look that bumpy on the way up and I never noticed the small trees either. I also give him a lot more credit for getting past the traffic as he cruised through the street below. As I write this today, with the blaring car horns, I still don't know how he managed to jump a curb, hang on and avoid traffic coming from both directions! Ben landed the wagon on our neighbor's lawn without a scratch on either himself or the wagon. Whew!

As I sprinted down the hill to congratulate Ben on the awesome test run, I figured out that wagons, hills and cars make a bad combination. The big problem that day was a combination of timing and birth order. Ben and I were gone a bit too long, and as I ran down the hill, I could see Mom in her panic-sprint darting up the sidewalk toward us. Mom's panic-sprint is

rather funny to watch. It is very similar to what a cat looks like when it accidentally falls in water. If Mom saw Ben's amazing driving skills firsthand, she did not appear as impressed as I was by the performance. I could see him smiling at first, but Ben's smile quickly turned to crocodile tears when he saw Mom's spastic dash to the scene.

The Lesson Learned

The wagon seemed a bit heavier as I pulled it home. Although Mom did not say a word on the walk, I learned that the fear of my punishment made things heavier — as if I was pulling a dump truck.

Mom's silence made me say dumb things too.

At first, I blurted, "We were really lucky no one

got hurt." Why did I say that? Maybe she didn't actually see Ben's journey down the hill and into the street. And then, when that did not get a response, I tried to appeal to her medical training, "I think I hurt my ankle on the way down the hill." Once again, nothing. Not even a glance.

Surprisingly, Mom did not yell at me much that day because she was busy wiping away Ben's fake tears and checking for

broken bones in various spots Ben now claimed hurt. To lighten the mood, I offered up my x-ray vision glasses to Mom, but she wasn't amused. I don't blame Ben for putting on a show. The punishment is always a little more bearable if one of us gets hurt — even fake.

My point here is that some activities are better done with your best friend instead of little brothers. After the incident, the wagon became a tool of torture for Saturday chores. Dad would force me to load dirt, carry sticks or bring things in and out of the garage with the wagon. Dad and I never talked about the wagon incident, but I knew he knew about it. And I know he knew I knew, if you know what I mean. I could hear him make odd comments to himself like, "This wagon looks *real* quick!" or "I wonder how fast this thing can go?" He clearly thought he was a funny guy. I never bother to respond to Dad's

odd comments because being a man means

keeping some of your thoughts to yourself.

A COUPLE MORE FISH
THAT GOT AWAY

The Cool Idea

Patrick James Thomas, the only person I know with three first names, has been my best friend for as long as I can remember. We all call him P.J. Although he doesn't have a lock on his bedroom door, P.J. has some pretty cool stuff in his room, including a drum set and an aquarium

filled with clownfish,

angelfish, and a bunch

of little black and silver

fish that swim around

in packs like little

piranha.

The Clown Fish

My favorite was the puffer fish. Although

it looked like a normal fish, when it was

frightened it would puff up into a much bigger

fish — like a balloon. I loved watching P.J.'s fish

after school. It was a

perfect way to avoid

my dreaded weekly

Chore Chart. Everyone

knows I can't have an

Angelfish

aquarium because my Dad is deathly allergic to

fish if they are in an aquarium (along with anything else you can put in aquariums like frogs, lizards, and snakes). Dad thinks it has something to do with a chemical reaction between these animals and the glass. This seems a bit strange to me but then again, I'm not a doctor.

The Big Problem

Watching P.J.'s fish was fun, but they went nuts when you played the drums. Tapping on the tank was even better because it made the fish flick in

different directions. Now that's entertainment!

On one particular day, I started tapping the tank with my finger, watching the fish jump around. Thinking that a louder tap might make the fish move faster, I started tapping with the drum sticks. Yep, a slightly different reaction. Using the drum sticks was easier because I could actually sit in a chair with my feet up next to the aquarium and tap away.

I've read that scientists think fish are mentally traumatized by people tapping on their tank. I can't imagine we will ever know the answer to this question until someone is able to talk to fish. For P.J.'s fish, the real trauma came when my tapping suddenly cracked the glass and made a perfectly round hole in the tank near the bottom.

At this point, water — a lot of water — starting pouring into P.J.'s bedroom.

When you first see a lot of water flooding into someone's bedroom, you immediately think about how to stop the water. In this case, I thought about using my hand. This was a really dumb move. In no time at all, there was water, fish and now blood flowing onto the floor from a rather large cut on my

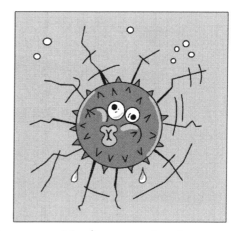

finger. Although it seemed to happen in slow motion, the water poured out quickly. I thought we had gotten lucky when the alarmed and inflated puffer fish stuffed the hole and stopped the water. But that was short-lived when it too

popped out. When it was all over, gallons and

gallons of water were making their way from

P.J.'s bedroom to the floor below. Any thought of

trying to clean

up the mess

and avoid

detection was

thwarted by

the fact that

P.J.'s dad just

so happened to be reading the newspaper —

right below us.

The Lesson Learned

I'm not sure if I passed out from the cut on

my finger or just the shock of what happened. It

might have been a natural defense mechanism to avoid further embarrassment. When I woke up, the fish were dead, P.J.'s dad was soaked, and my cut finger was throbbing. As I walked home that evening, I felt pretty bad.

By the time I arrived home, Mom had the first aid kit

out and was ready for action. After explaining the horror of what happened to Mom and Dad, I told them I was sure glad we didn't have a fish tank. After giving Dad a weird look, Mom said we were lucky Dad had the aquarium allergy. I agreed.

Dad called Mr. Thomas and promised to head to Hal's Hardware Store to get supplies to help him patch the hole in the ceiling. Mom and I found a coupon in the *Herald* for $5.00 off anything at Pet Planet so we picked out a new aquarium for P.J. While we were there, I also grabbed a flyer for the annual Pet Planet Pond Pick Up — a Horn Hill event where we get together to clean up Croaker Pond for future generations. Maybe Dad and I could get some fishing in after the clean-up. P.J.'s dad appeared ready for some new fish when we arrived with the new tank.

"I heard you were coming over today, Jeffrey!"

Men make big mistakes and even bigger
messes. As you can see, it takes teamwork to
clean them up. The really big messes require the
help of experienced professionals. Let me
introduce you to some of Horn Hill's best.

THE GENERATION GAP

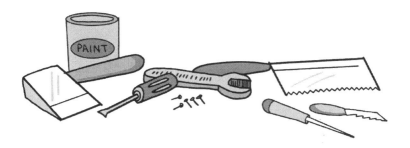

The Cool Idea

"Jeffrey, we're going to the store! Please get in the car!"

The shopping trip. Is there anything more painful to a kid at the outset of his manhood? Don't my parents remember the ketchup incident? Haven't they learned that nothing good can come from bringing me on these boring trips? (In case you were wondering, the answers are no, no and NO!) Frankly, based on the wagon

incident, I wasn't safe near anything with wheels

prior to becoming a man.

But then there is the trip to Hal's

Hardware Store. I never mind a trip to Hal's

because it is a man's gold mine! Everything you've

ever wanted to touch but aren't allowed to even

glance too long at in your home is up for grabs at

Hal's. And I mean *everything!* Are you looking for

a hammer? Well, you need to pick it up to see if it

feels right, don't you? Drills, tape measures,

screwdrivers, wrenches,

nails, nuts, bolts, and

gadgets of all kinds are

fair game. Hal's even has

a section of "See It On TV" treasures! And then

there is Hal and his team of old men who patrol

the aisles. They love talking about tools and, as

Hal says in his commercials, "Only the best can

wear Hal's vest!"

TEAM HAL
"Only the best can wear Hal's vest!"

Dad seems to enjoy taking me to Hal's as

much as I like going. I'm not positive, but I think

hardware stores seem to be a central element of

man training.

I remember so many great trips to Hal's. And one that was not so great. Dad really wasn't good at keeping an eye on me. As I ran down the aisles at Hal's, I would often hear, "DON'T TOUCH THE TOOLS!" from three aisles away — a direct order any young man can understand.

But sometimes Dad yelled out, "DON'T LET ME CATCH YOU TOUCHING THE TOOLS!" while I was inspecting something I thought we might need for a project. I'm not some type of delinquent, so I did, in fact, consider my dad's words before I dove into my ongoing investigations. On this particular day, after thinking about it, I concluded Dad was challenging me. This was a test. After all, I had heard these words many times before — like when he told me not to let him catch me eating more candy before dinner. "Got it, Dad! I won't let you catch me!" Weird instructions, but man training doesn't always make sense.

Well, game on! I won't let you catch me taking a better look at this chain saw. But I still needed to figure out exactly what this machine was all about. With the added pressure of not getting caught, I carefully lifted the chain saw off the rack and began my thorough examination.

The Big Problem

"GET YOUR HANDS AWAY FROM THE

CHAIN SAW!" If you are caught with your hand

in, let's say, a candy jar, your hand can be quickly

removed (while sneaking a piece of candy if

you're really good). Unlike a candy jar, being

startled

with a chain

saw in your

hands

doesn't

allow you

to slither away as easily as you might hope under

the same circumstances. Quickly moving your

hands from a chain saw causes problems. This is

especially true when the chain saw is slightly bigger than you.

Dad caught me. Although I was certainly upset that I failed in my dad's challenge, I think the pain I was feeling was coming from my finger which was sliced by the chain saw blade. Why

didn't he just tell me not to touch it in the first place?

The Lesson Learned

Ketchup and blood do look a lot alike. Unlike my mom, Team Hal knew the difference right away. I think they must get special training that nurses don't get. Hal and his team were really nice to us. After bandaging my finger, they even gave me a

coveted Hal's Hardware light bulb balloon and a realistic Hal's name badge. Dad filled out a bunch of paperwork about where we live and why he was not watching me carefully. While Dad was filling out the forms, I explained to Hal the game my dad and I were playing. He chuckled and told me a lot of dads play the same game with their sons at his store. After Dad finished filling out his confession, neither of us was in a shopping mood, so we left.

On the way home, Dad explained that the phrase, "Don't let me catch you" was not actually a game at all despite what Hal had told me. Apparently, the phrase means the same thing as "Do not touch." Go figure. I tried to explain to him why that was a bit confusing, but he didn't seem to understand. Since Hal and I certainly get it, Dad must be a part of this generation gap that I hear people talk about all the time.

It was some time before Dad and I went to Hal's again. When we finally did go back to get the supplies to fix P.J.'s ceiling, Hal's team recognized us right away. They walked around with my dad and me, and it seemed like there was someone to help us around every corner. They were really nice about the whole thing. Team Hal knows that one of the keys to manhood is sticking together — even when accidents happen.

MANHOLES

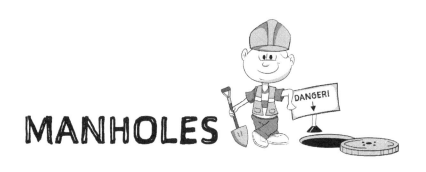

THE TOOLS OF MANHOOD

At the entrance to Hal's Hardware is this picture of Hal:

And, of course, to create the future a man needs tools. What kind of tools? All kinds. In this installment of Manholes, let's look at the top ten tools every boy needs to have in his tool bag to become a man. These are the tools you need to avoid all sorts of Manholes. Get your tools and create your future!

10.   **Work Boots**. A man must be prepared for the hard work ahead of him. Safety first!

9.   **Deodorant.** Because creating the future should never result in a funny smell.

8.   **A LONG Tape Measure.** The rule is "measure twice, cut once." Even if you never follow the rule, it sure is fun to stretch out a tape measure and let it snap back into its case!

7.   **Lubricant.** Because changes should never make a sound unless you want them to.

6.   **Band Aids.**

Sometimes change hurts.

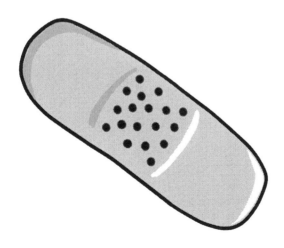

5.   A Fire Extinguisher.

When change gets out of hand . . .

4.   **A Swiss Army Knife.** When you don't know what tool you need to make a change, the Swiss Army has your back.

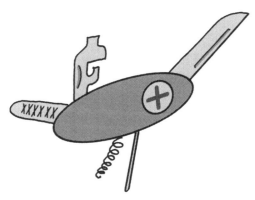

3.   **A Hammer.** A great hammer changes everything.

2.   **A Smile.** A great smile changes everything and EVERYONE!

And last but not least . . .

1. **A Lucky Rabbit's Foot.** When none of your other tools work.

And when the top ten tools don't work, it's

back to Hal's!

SAVE $5 ON A FIX
FOR YOUR NEXT MISTAKE!

THE POLITE GENTLEMAN

The Cool Idea

Every

couple of

months my

Grandma

Bonnie comes

for a visit.

After dealing

with the sloppy kisses she always dishes out, we

actually have a great time because she plays

board games with us and always gives us cool

stuff. The last time she came was for my

birthday, and she gave me a digital camera and a

roll of dimes. Grandma Bonnie also tells us funny

stories about the olden days and what Mom was

like when she was a little girl. I'm not positive, but

from listening to Grandma Bonnie all these years,

I think Mom wore a

lot of white

clothes when she

was young, and

she floated

around on a cloud.

She may have even

had wings.

The Big Problem

For some reason, Grandma Bonnie likes to

tease Dad. Just like Mom when she is driving us

kids in the car, Grandma Bonnie mumbles odd

comments to herself — especially when Dad is

nearby. Dad brought in his dress shirts from the dry cleaners one afternoon, and I heard Grandma Bonnie say quietly, "Real men know how to use an iron." Whenever Grandma Bonnie starts mumbling, Dad always responds with a smile and the same polite comment,

You know what they say Grandma Bonnie: Behind every successful man is a proud wife and a surprised mother-in-law!

I always wonder how Dad does it. If it were me, I would get pretty ticked off at Grandma. Instead, he just smiles. I've heard him say many times he deserves an Academy Award. When I ask what he

means, Dad's explanation is always the same: "A polite gentleman is a man who knows how to play the accordion, but doesn't." Huh?

The Lesson Learned

I'm not sure what Dad means, but his reaction to Grandma Bonnie makes me think about when funny things happen to other people that require the polite gentleman to refrain from laughing (no matter how funny he finds it). Interestingly, I think all of these examples could be Academy Award- winning Hollywood hits . . . co-starring the polite

gentleman, of course. I decided to put pen to paper and make some movie posters.

Mom and Dad exchange gross kisses
while in public

Mr. Thomas thinks he is still the same size
he was in college

Ben puking because he ate too much
Halloween candy

Kate putting on too much make-up for a date

I left my drawings out in the den one night.

The next morning, while I was cleaning up my

mess, I noticed there was one more:

Dad is pretty funny sometimes. In the movie of life, being a man means keeping your sense of humor no matter what happens.

BUY ONE, GET THIRTEEN FREE!

The Cool Idea

P.J. and I have an agreement that if something cool one of us owns is at risk of being stolen, seized or otherwise harmed, we will give it to the other for safekeeping. I'm not sure why, but we call it "Option 48." So, for example, when Kate showed a bit too much interest in my football jersey last fall, I called P.J. and did an Option 48 on it immediately. I kept it at P.J.'s house and went to his house when I wanted to wear it. That's what best friends do for one another.

Did your dad wear my jersey when I left it at your house?

One Saturday morning, we were riding in the back seat of my mom's car on the way to Pondview Mall. We were snickering about what might be the biggest Option 48 of our friendship. Although she didn't know why on earth we wanted to go with her that morning, after a standard pat-down for ketchup packets and other explodable devices, she let us come.

She parked the car and once we'd

confirmed

a meeting

place and

time, we were off. P.J. and I raced through the

mall and soon came face to face with our latest

obsession at Pet Planet — the hamster.

What an odd looking creature! It's the size of a mouse, but much furrier with only a stump for a tail. It looks just like a miniature teddy bear. If that's not enough to make you want one, it actually stuffs food in its cheeks to save for later, which is what life is all about, right? Clearly, we needed one. With the twenty bucks I found in the couch burning a hole in my pocket, we were closer than ever to making our dream come true.

But what color? Brown? White? Orange? White and orange? We looked at them all for awhile. As we debated the pros and cons of each color, we blurted out at the same time, "Let's just get the fat one!" After taking my cash and sliding our hamster into what looked like a Happy Meal box, the man at the counter looked at us funny

when we

asked for a

brown

paper bag.

He dug one

out for us, and we raced out of the store with

Pudge, our new hamster. As we sat in the middle

of Pond View Mall waiting for my mom, P.J. and I

made a list of things we needed to do when we

got back home. P.J. would bring over his old

patched up aquarium (since it couldn't hold fish

anymore) and we would set up the tank in my

room. If my parents told me Pudge could not

stay, we would Option 48 him to P.J.'s house

because his mom was a big sucker for cute

animals. P.J. had already hinted to his mom that he might be getting one from a friend who could not keep it. Genius, right?

"What did you boys find?" P.J. and I both jumped out of our seats when my mom showed up even though we were expecting her.

"Oh, I got treats for Charlie and P.J. bought some toys for his cat Tiger," I blurted out. We tried not to talk much on the way home because we both knew we would end up giggling like Kate and her friends reading a new issue of *Teen Throb* magazine. The only time we talked was when the hamster started scratching at the box and we needed to cover up the noise.

The Big Problem

Despite our well-laid plans, it did not take Ben long to ruin them. After P.J. and I set up the tank, Ben burst into my room. Before we could even begin to negotiate with him, Ben was screaming down the hallway (with a few less clothes) ready to tell anyone he could about the new addition to the family.

We immediately began Option 48

procedures. But as we were packing, my dad

came in with Ben. Surprisingly, after we gave Ben

his clothes back, Dad took an interest in Pudge.

Dad did not seem startled by Pudge and he didn't

seem at all concerned about his aquarium allergy

as he picked Pudge up to take a closer look. It

didn't take much coaxing to convince Dad to let

us keep him because, as he said, "One hamster isn't going to cause any problems." We played with Pudge for the rest of the day and P.J. slept over. Even Charlie seemed pleased with our purchase.

Pudge wore out *her* welcome rather quickly. Pudge and thirteen Pudgies were in the tank when I woke up. Pudge had somehow replicated herself ... *thirteen times!* Ben came in to see Pudge and once again he was off to the races screaming down the hall when he saw the new additions. Ben came back with Dad, who didn't seem to be confused at all about what had happened. Without explaining anything, he gave P.J. and I the "serious" look and said we would need to discuss how I was going to solve this misunderstanding. I could have one hamster and no more.

The Lesson Learned

I ended up keeping Pudge. P.J. took two Pudgies. Dad took P.J. and I to Pet Planet and they bought the eleven other Pudgies back from me for the price I paid for Pudge. They even gave P.J. and me some free hamster chew sticks. Just like me, Dad saw the flyer for The Pet Planet Pond Pick Up and smiled as he grabbed one like he had some big plans.

Pudge has been great entertainment for us. We set her cage up like a movie set, and as she wanders through the cage, it looks like a giant bear is attacking a city!

The lesson? The lesson learned is that fat hamsters have the amazing ability to replicate overnight! And that this is absolutely *awesome!* Oh, and I learned my dad really doesn't have an aquarium allergy. He apparently received a vaccination years ago for it and didn't tell Mom. So, Dad is in the dog house with Mom for hiding something. As I see it, if Dad had not pretended to still have the aquarium allergy, I would have never needed to sneak a hamster into the house. I think Dad and I both learned that in manhood, honesty is the best policy to avoid these little misunderstandings.

SAVING MAJOR MATT MASON

The Cool Idea

If you need a break, take one now. This will
be one of the most difficult chapters of *The
Manhood Manual*, but I think you are ready for
"The Talk." You've learned quite a few lessons,
but NONE will be as important as this one.

Typically, your dad will sit you down to talk about this because it is *that* important. You will sweat. He will sweat. You both will be very nervous and confused. Your mom will never fully understand because she is, after all, not a man. This is by far one of the biggest hurdles to your manhood. Have you figured it out yet? No, not *that!* (Gross, by the way!)

Since you are not the man I am today, I'm sure you are thinking to yourself, "Okay, Jeffrey is just crazy. I understand fire and I can handle it." Trust me, you don't, and you can't. I learned my first lesson about the dangers of fire with Sam Schlister. Unfortunately, my dad's collector G.I. Joe action figure paid a horrible price. This is my painful story.

Sam Schlister lives on the next block and is three years older than me. Before I became a man, I thought Sam was a lot smarter than me because that's what he told me. One afternoon, while G.I. Joe and my dad's coveted Major Matt Mason action figure were on a secret mission behind our garage, Sam spotted me and slinked over. He told me that my dad's action figures

were made of a special material designed to withstand realistic war conditions. I really didn't believe him and I told him so. Naturally, he wanted to prove it to me. I'm not sure why, but I agreed to let him.

Sam went home and returned a short time later with a tiny yellow plastic container and some matches. The container clearly said "lighter fluid," but it looked like water to me. It smelled funny. Sam sprayed the liquid on the G.I. Joe my dad referred to as "Man of Action." Sam lit a match and, as he held the now damp G.I. Joe, he told me to pretend to spray him with the flame thrower. Awesome idea, right?

The Big Problem

Sam Schlister is a great big moron. Man of

Action was not fireproof —

not even close. Sam dropped Man of Action and

watched him burn. After the clothes burned off

poor Joe, the black smoke from his plastic body

burning got pretty thick. I watched in shock and

didn't know what to do. As the flames and smoke

died down,

Man of

Action had

become a

puddle of

plastic. At that point, I realized that Sam was

long gone. I took what remained of my dad's

collection and pretended to play for awhile in my

room. I knew I needed to deal with Sam's stupidity. I went back behind the garage and inspected the horrible mess.

Although the smoke had cleared, Dad's G.I. Joe was now just a plastic puddle with chunks of stuff that didn't quite melt all the way. I definitely saw a hand and a boot, but everything else was a blob. G.I. Joe was now G.I. Blob and worse yet, it was stuck to the concrete walk that went around the garage. I couldn't scrape it off, so I did the only thing I could — I plopped a metal bucket on top of it with a note to try and distract anyone who came across it.

I knew Kate wasn't going to go back behind the garage, and if anyone else found it, they would hopefully blame Kate for the mess. I really think I'm a genius sometimes when it comes to getting out of jams like this.

The Lesson Learned

Well, Dad clearly didn't fall for the note. But he did find the strength to peel G.I. Blob off the concrete. Dad discovered the mess on one of his "Surveys of the Crandle Kingdom," as he refers to his walks in the backyard

after dinner. Dad must have been in shock when he found G.I. Blob because he didn't say a word when he came in my bedroom with the blob and the bucket in his hands. I immediately blamed it on Sam. Dad told me that whatever happened, it was my job to look after something that was not mine and I had failed miserably.

Obviously, I learned Sam Schlister is a great big moron. That night, I returned the rest of Dad's box of action figures to him. I could tell he was just as sad as I was about it. Dad let me keep Major Matt Mason and told me to take care of him because he was the most valuable action figure he had left.

Being a man isn't an age thing. Part of becoming a man is making good decisions. From that horrible day forward, Major Matt Mason stayed in Fort Box and only came out for special missions. Although boys like Sam Schlister find burning stuff fun, men find *keeping* stuff more fun. For some weird reason, after the Major Matt Mason incident, I caught the urge to collect things. But that's a story for later.

MANHOLES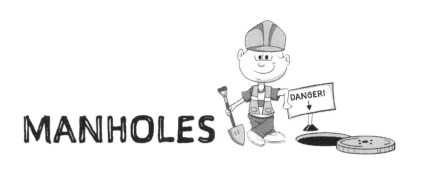

DANGER EVERYWHERE!

When you become a man, you know to steer

away from all the dumb and dangerous activities

you did as a boy. As Sam Schlister the moron

showed me, fire qualifies as both dumb *and*

dangerous. But trust me, there are many other

dangers lurking out there. In this installment of

Manholes, Police Chief Stevens and I will review

just a few of the dangers I've been *unable* to

avoid. With our help, hopefully you can do better.

You can really get hooked on skateboarding.

"Extreme swinging" is not an actual sport for a reason.

A key part of any tree house design is a way to get down.

Our teachers always say we need to "learn to soar".

Boys like to test the limits of spatial reality.

Over the years, Police Chief Stevens and I have made a great team on my travels into manhood.

COLLECTING TROUBLE

The Cool Idea

As I mentioned, I'm not sure why, but men like to collect stuff. As you know, Dad collects unmelted action figures from when he was a kid. When he isn't fishing, my grandpa loves looking at his collection of "Coins from Around the Globe" as he proudly refers to them. At P.J.'s house, football trading cards are king. P.J. and his Dad spend hours comparing uniforms over the years, studying stats and figuring out if any of the cards are worth some cash. My Uncle Bob's collection is a bit strange. He likes to put together jigsaw puzzles, glue them to a board and display

them like artwork. I think this is why Uncle Bob is single and lives alone. All of these collectibles have one thing in common:

THEY ARE BORING!

So, on the path to my manhood, I must learn to collect things. But what? I'm interested in a lot of stuff like rocks, bugs, and video games, but I don't think that collecting any of them would be particularly fun. My weekly allowance, even after my raise, doesn't really bring in bags of cash. So I can't collect coins, sport cards or dolls (er, I mean action figures, Dad). P.J.'s dad suggested I collect dead fish, but I think he was kidding. Honestly, if I'm going to collect something, I want to turn it up a notch if you know what I mean. I want to collect something nobody else is collecting. I really enjoy bugging my sister Kate. Could there be something collectible with this? Probably not.

Or is there?

Remember that digital camera Grandma
Bonnie gave me for my birthday? After months
of wondering what on earth I was going to do
with it, I stumbled upon my new hobby. I decided I
would collect memorable photographs. Not just
any photographs, mind you, but photographs of
anything in my life I found worthy of
documenting. So that means *everything!*

I started with some pretty funny shots. P.J. and I took great action photos of us at the park. Sometimes we went to the mall and photographed ourselves as mannequins. We even got Charlie in on the fun.

At P.J.'s prompting, I took my hobby from funny to hilarious. Pictures of Kate when she first woke up in the  morning were instant classics in my collection. Snapshots of Kate after being scared beyond belief were pretty funny too. When photos of Kate got old, I moved on to Ben — and even Mom and Dad. My collectible family photos were

awesome! With P.J. as my eager assistant, the

results were amazing.

After our photo shoots, P.J. and I would

retire to my room, lock the door and download

our photos. We would then carefully review and

select the best ones to include in *The*

UNAUTHORIZED Crandle Family Photo Album.

The album was stored securely in Fort Box.

The Big Problem

Some things in life are just strange. I cannot think of any event my mom and dad don't consider worthy of a photo. And Kate just loves posting goofy photos to Facebook to share with her universe of weird friends. Given everyone's love of photos, I'm not sure why my family didn't support my new hobby. I mean, it's not like anyone knew about The *UNAUTHORIZED Crandle Family Photo Album*. I'm not sure when P.J. and I crossed the line, but I know exactly what we were doing when my family decided to get their revenge.

In our playroom we have a large chest filled with old Halloween costumes. One boring, rainy afternoon, P.J. and I were rummaging around looking for costumes to try out for our next photo shoot. A couple of dares later and we both ended up in princess gowns and crowns. Funny? You bet! We promised each other no photos. As we laughed hysterically and checked ourselves out in the mirror, our laughter turned to panic when Kate burst into the room with *her* camera. Within sixty seconds the screaming and shouting brought my entire family to the playroom.

The Lesson Learned

When the battle was over, I could tell by the

smile on Dad's face that P.J. and I were not going

to win an argument over the photos that were

now inside the camera in my sister's grubby

hands. I immediately resorted to fake crying, but

because P.J. was with me, I couldn't really give my

best performance. I then realized what I had

done. I didn't leave someone behind to support

me. It dawned on me that taking the picture of Dad picking his nose was probably not the brightest idea. I could have avoided the photos of Mom reading her self-help books with her beauty mask on. Maybe I should have left Mom and Dad out of the photos entirely to ensure some unbiased parenting in this type of situation. But no, I couldn't help myself and now P.J. and I were at the mercy of whatever twisted justice was about to be handed down.

My dad pointed his finger at the both of us and let us have it in the worst way possible. "Jeffrey, you have taken too many photos of your sister, your brother, and even your mother and me over the past several months, and I'll bet you have kept all of the ones that make us look absolutely silly. So, I think Kate can take a look at her photos and keep one of her favorites."

It didn't take long for our photo to get on Kate's Facebook page for the universe of her dork friends to see. After carefully selecting and presenting Kate with the threat of some of my better photos of her, Kate decided to take down ours. Our photo circulated on the World Wide Web for less than a day. Hopefully nobody saw it or saved it.

For you girls reading this, manhood is definitely about collecting things ... other than the trouble I seem to collect. For the boys out there, I know you're now wondering if becoming a man is about getting even with your sister. I'm not sure, but we'll definitely find out.

CASH ON DELIVERY

The Cool Idea

Next to fire, the biggest hurdle on the journey to manhood is money. You know, legal tender, the green stuff, dough, dinero, bread, chicken feed, cabbage, coinage, wampum, scratch . . . cold, hard cash. If you've got it, you want to spend it. And even if you don't have it, banks will give you magical plastic cards with money in them to use. And sometimes, if you're too young to get a magical plastic card, companies that really,

really want to sell you something will send you

the stuff with your promise to pay them when

the stuff gets delivered to your house.

"Wait! What?" I hear you all saying.

Yeah, C.O.D. Cash on Delivery. You think I'm

kidding? I'm not. With revenge on my mind for a

horrible Facebook post of P.J and me in dresses, I

showed P.J. this ad in the *Horn Hill Herald*

classifieds:

We did some research on the C.O.D. program and it seemed legit. Now, we just needed to be at home when the mailman arrived. We did some more digging and we figured out that you can track packages

online and the post office will notify you by email when your package will arrive. That was great, but the mail comes to both my house and P.J.'s house before school gets out. Then P.J. noticed you can choose guaranteed 3-day delivery — *including Saturdays!* We placed our online order on a Wednesday and received the notice: Guaranteed Delivery on Saturday. All we needed was a good cover. We decided on a classic: the lemonade stand.

The Big Problem

On Saturday P.J. and I prepared for the shipment. We dug out the red wagon and a small table, declaring our intention to earn some extra money. Although Kate expressed suspicion, Mom and Dad were pleased with our "initiative" and Mom even helped us get set up at the end of the driveway *right next to the mailbox!* P.J. made a sign that was perfect for the occasion.

It was a warm day and sales were rather brisk at twenty-five cents a glass. In fact, they were too brisk. We were making some serious coin and attracting too much traffic. We were having problems keeping up with demand, so we

needed to bring in a partner. Ben was an eager

helper. We told him we would pay him $1.50 for his

time and he gladly accepted the offer. Mom and

Dad were once again pleased — this time with

our "teamwork." They left us alone.

When we saw the mailman coming up the

street, we put our new plan into place. We jacked

up the price of lemonade thinking nobody would

be interested in buying. Unfortunately, Ben was

telling people it was a mistake and still bringing in

the customers. This is when our other partner

woke up and solved the problem. Charlie decided

he was thirsty and knocked our table over.

By the time the mailman came, we had one

cup of lemonade left . . . for him. We told him we

were his C.O.D. delivery and he was happy to

settle up with us while enjoying his lemonade. To

my folks, it must have looked like he was paying

for lemonade.

The big problem? Ben. To our never-silent partner, it looked too suspicious. Ben saw it all and was standing there wide-eyed and confused. P.J. and I prepared to give chase, but Ben had a surprise for us.

The Lesson Learned

I'm not sure when boys start thinking about money, but it starts at about age eight in my family. Unlike when he first saw Pudge, Ben did not run to tell anyone. He looked at P.J. and me, glanced at the lemonade money, and gazed back at us smiling. We asked him how much. He saw an opportunity and went for it — he demanded it all. We looked at the box of Famous Ivan's Itching Powder, and P.J. and I agreed that this was worth it. We gave him all of the money . . . with a modest condition attached to it.

Mom and Dad were a bit confused by the entire afternoon. P.J. and I considered the day a big success. We talked about how great it was that Ben was becoming a man. We then went outside and planned how we would show Kate the power of Famous Ivan's.

STINKIFICATION

The Cool Idea

My sister Kate serves as a daily reminder that girls stink. Early on, I could handle her skipping instead of walking everywhere the family

went

together.

And I

didn't mind Kate sometimes enlisting Major Matt Mason (before the fire incident) for a tea party now and then. When Kate changed her name to Unicornia and didn't respond to her real name for a month, that was okay too, because I really didn't want to talk to her anyway. P.J. and I refer

Unicornia

to Kate's ability to annoy us as "stinkification."

These days, Kate takes stinkification up a notch.

From spending hours in the bathroom or walking

around the house video-chatting when she isn't,

Kate is *always* annoying. When her friends come

over, the stinkification

gets exponentially

worse. No matter the

season, they always

take out Kate's big pink

blanket, cuddle up and

giggle. A jiggling, giggling pink blob of girls! Ugh!

The pink blob is at its worst when watching TV. They watch an endless string of movies about the journey of a nerdy, unpopular girl in high school who has a secret crush on a popular boy and must overcome a gang of cheerleaders to finally date this dreamy boy. I mean how many of these movies can there be out there?!? And how many can you watch?!?

After the Facebook photo incident, tensions were high. P.J. and I knew it was time to fight back the day we came home to play Men of War, our new favorite video game, only to find the pink blob watching movies. We asked the pink blob nicely several times to let us play. It laughed

and told us we should just look at the box and
pretend we were playing the game in our heads.
Oh yeah? At that point, P.J. and I decided it was
time to become Men of War. A full frontal attack
against four (possibly more) teenage girls in a
pink blanket was not the right strategy. We were
not going to defeat the pink blob that way. The
only obvious choice for P.J. and I was a delayed
flank attack with Famous Ivan's Itching Powder.
The time was now!

The next day we carefully loaded up the pink blanket with a healthy shake of Famous Ivan's. Then, we folded it back up and returned it to a small basket near the T.V. The next time Kate and her friends

came over to watch a movie, Famous Ivan's would do its work and teach them all an important lesson!

The Big Problem

I arrived home from school the next week and looked in the family room with shades drawn to find the pink blob watching TV. I remember it well because the pink blob was watching an update on Kate's new favorite boy band Hot Rush. Jackpot!! That did not take long at all! I called P.J. and told him to come over. When P.J. arrived, we snuck behind the couch to watch Famous Ivan's work its magic. As we quietly snickered, we wondered how many girls were in the blob and whether Kate would start calling friends over to join them.

And then it happened . . .

A sneeze, followed by another sneeze, and yet another. There is only one person in my family who always sneezes three times . . .and it isn't Kate! As the couch shook, P.J. and I froze.

The Lesson Learned

You can never really predict when someone in your family is going to get sick. It is also hard to picture someone like your dad wrapping himself up in a pink blanket and watching TV all day when he is sick. And who knew he liked Hot

Rush too? So imagine my surprise when it turned

out it was Dad bundled up just inches from us,

overdosing on

Famous Ivan's

Itching Powder.

As I write

this, I'm back in

my room. I think

P.J. might still be behind the couch. It has been

two days since Dad's run-in with Famous Ivan's. I

just pulled a second candy bar out of Fort Box.

I'm not sure, but I think Dad has been in the

shower for about an hour today again. It would

appear that the rash from Famous Ivan's comes

and goes. Every time it comes back, I end up back

in my room.

None of this would have happened but for

one thing. That thing is Kate — and the

stinkification of our home with her loud,

obnoxious friends! For this reason, sisters rank

at number three on the hurdles to overcome to

get to manhood — right behind fire and money.

MANHOLES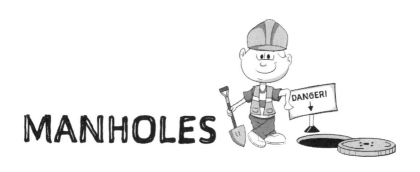

THE SELFIE

As I've proven, photos can be giant manholes for boys. But then there is the selfie. Ah, the many faces of manhood! Some are happy. Some are sad. All of them are impossible to forget. It's my belief that you need to experience most of the faces of manhood before you can really call yourself a man.

Mischievous

Embarrassed

Anxious

Disgusted

Scared

Confident

Confused

Let's add your very own manhood selfie
right here!

YOU!

YOU!

PET PLANET POND PICK UP

The Cool Idea

Taking a break from the challenges of

becoming a man is ironically a key to manhood.

Every year, P.J and I go with our dads to the

annual Pet Planet Pond

Pick Up. The year I lost my

XPX 2000, Ben decided

to come too. Although

there was no

motivational speech or

list of pond pick up

fundamentals, Dad put

on his painfully embarrassing "Clean Rivers And

Ponds Society" t-shirt and gathered supplies like

he was going on a safari. I was ready to go well before Dad. And yes, we packed the poles in case we had time to fish.

As Mr. Thomas and my Dad led the way to Croaker Pond, P.J. and I pulled Ben and the supplies in the red wagon. We passed Horn Hill and Ben started telling P.J. about the time we'd put the wagon through its paces. He gave us the play-by-play of that wicked ride, and I chimed in with my imitation of

Mom's panic-sprint. P.J. and I were laughing so hard we fell behind Dad and Mr. Thomas.

The Big Problem

When we arrived at Croaker Pond, P.J. and I grabbed our trash bags and started picking up trash as we went. Ben caught on quickly under our tutelage. Ben had our bag full of trash by the time we arrived at the spot of the "XPX 2000 incident." We took a break under the tree where

Dad had been sleeping that day. As I started to retell the fateful story to Ben and P.J., Ben headed down to the shore to look around. He noticed a frog in Croaker Pond which was no real surprise — it is Croaker Pond

after all. But this big frog seemed to be stuck on

a rock with his back leg wrapped in string.

We decided to help this poor frog out

despite it being a bit far out in the pond. We

made kind of a human rope, but we weren't quite

long enough. Mr. Thomas and Dad saw us and

walked over to yell at us. Once they saw what

was going on, they decided to help too. With Mr.

Thomas and Dad at the end, we stretched out to

the rock. Ben was on the end, and I held him as he

tried to untie the string from the frog's leg. Just then, the frog hopped on top of me, and the string pulled what appeared to be a large stick up from the water. The frog then hopped on to P.J., and I realized that the big stick was my XPX 2000! Ben tried to grab it and, just as he did, the frog jumped again, this time onto Mr. Thomas. I grabbed the pole and fell into the water. Everyone else soon followed. The frog jumped free and my XPX 2000 was now in my hands!

As I cleaned it off, I started to get a tug on the end of the line. Could it be? No, it couldn't. Or could it? I started reeling in the line. Something was fighting on the other end. After struggling for a few minutes, I saw the monster fish! It jumped out of the water and this time everyone saw it. He was still on the end of my pole! Right

after he dove back in, I tugged a little harder and

the line snapped . . .

The Lesson Learned

Mr. Thomas, Dad, P.J. and Ben all looked at

me in shock. Before we could even climb out of

Croaker Pond, we all looked at each other and at

the same time all cried, "NOW THAT WAS A

MONSTER FISH!"

A *Horn Hill Herald* reporter was at Croaker

Pond taking pictures of the event that day.

Unfortunately, Police Chief Stevens was there

too. With the *Herald* reporter looking on and

snapping photos of the entire incident, Chief

Stevens decided that rules were rules. Since we

were swimming in the pond, he would need to

bring us in for booking. As we climbed out of Croaker Pond, we told him the story about the monster fish and the frog we saved, but he wasn't buying it. Despite the pleas of Mr. Thomas and my Dad, Chief Stevens was arresting us!

We were all fingerprinted, photographed and officially booked. We were Horn Hill's newest perps! Mom and Kate picked us up, and we could tell Mom was not happy. She said that the *Horn Hill Herald* had been calling looking for more dirt on the families caught swimming in Croaker Pond instead of cleaning it up! I really didn't care what would be reported in the paper. We knew the real story and with the XPX 2000 back home, Dad and I were a bit closer to catching the monster fish! Dad didn't seem too upbeat about the whole situation. He said he might get kicked out of the Clean Rivers and Ponds Society for this little ordeal. And even though Dad is the Editor-in-Chief of *The Horn Hill Herald*, the reporters wouldn't sugarcoat this incident in the paper.

It was a dark day for the Crandle family. It seems that men sometimes get in trouble for no other reason

than, well, that we're men! Maybe there's nothing we can do about it, and being a man means living with this simple fact of life.

THE SUNDAY PAPER

The VERY Cool Idea

Although it might not make complete sense

quite yet, I hope you soon agree that this is the

one and only book that can help you get to where

I am today — a successful, well-adjusted, good

looking, thirteen-year-old MAN! My cool idea

was to share some of my stories and secrets to

becoming a man and, if you've paid attention,

you're *almost* there.

The Big Problem

But before we get there, I suppose you

want to know what happened the day *after* the

Pet Planet Pond Pick Up. Well, there it was, on the

front page of the *Horn Hill Herald (below the*

fold as Dad stresses):

**HORN HILL HERALD EDITOR-IN-CHIEF
ARRESTED AT PET PLANET POND PICK UP!!**

The article was actually pretty cool. It described how the President of C.R.A.P.S. (my dad), along with his family and friends, saved a frog before falling into the pond and being arrested. The article explained that the entire arrest was a big misunderstanding and Police Chief Stevens publicly apologized for the entire ordeal. According to the article, Dad has been doing the Croaker Pond clean up (before Pet Planet sponsored it) with friends and family for over twenty years, long before I was even born! Who knew!?!

Now that I'm a man, Dad and I like to sit and read the *Herald* on Sunday mornings. Over the years, we've searched for new fishing poles, priced new cars for Mom, found jobs, and clipped coupons for Hal's Hardware Store. We even catch up on the news! There is something for everyone in the Sunday edition of the *Herald*. Mom loves cutting coupons and Kate needs the fashion tips. Ben likes the Sunday paper because he can make very large paper airplanes. By Sunday afternoon, even Charlie figures out a way to get wrapped up in the news of the day. As I was wiping some of Charlie's drool off the paper, it finally dawned on me that becoming a man maybe wasn't as hard as I thought it would be.

The HUGE Lesson Learned

P.J came over the Sunday after the Pet Planet Pond Pick Up. As we sat and looked at the front page photo, the whole family was laughing. Even Dad was starting to smile about it. Mom and Kate still didn't believe the story about the monster fish. Then we turned to the Trophy Tales, like we always do, to look at the catch of the week. There it was, another photo of us at the Croaker Pond right as Police Chief Stevens showed up.

**ONE TEAM FOUND AN OLD FISHING POLE
WHILE CLEANING UP CROAKER POND**

There is a big manhood lesson to be learned

from the Sunday paper after all. Each and every

Sunday, no matter the season, you can turn to

the back of the Sports section and look at the

Trophy Tales. You will find pictures of real men

smiling from ear to ear. These men are with their

fish and, more often than not, they are also with

a grandpa, a dad, brother, a son, a best friend, or

even their mom, sister or daughter. Regardless of who is with them or the size of their catch, they all have a great big smile. Much bigger than the pretend smile you throw on for school photos or the one that is quickly erased right after your crazy Grandma Bonnie kisses you. These smiles are different.

After seeing our photo in Trophy Tales, I realized I was trying too hard to become a man. I was probably too reckless with my little brother (and our wagon), too careless with my best friend's fish, too bold at Hal's Hardware Store, and certainly way too crazy trying to get even with my sister Kate. The list is much longer, but you get the idea.

Being a man is being happy with the little things in life and laughing even if the big one gets away. The big one might be a monster fish, but oftentimes it is something else. The big one might be letting down your dad when he gives you his action figure collection to play with. It might be even bigger, like the test you studied for and failed, not making the team you tried super hard to be on, or not getting the part you wanted in the school play.

The fact is that sometimes you miss the great people in your life and the awesome stuff that is happening all around you when you are striving so hard to be a man. The people in Trophy Tales every week all have one thing in common . . . they're enjoying the journey!

Enjoy your journey!

WAIT! EPI-WHAT?!?

Hey, you're not done with this book yet!

The devil is in the details, remember?!? You need

to make *The Manhood Manual* your very own.

Don't worry, I will walk you through this. First,

we'll add *your* stories to *The Manhood Manual*.

Second, we'll start your list of Fort Box items.

Finally, I've created a secret letter for you to

finish so you can share *The Manhood Manual*

with a friend or younger brother.

 If you can't part with your copy of *The*

Manhood Manual, visit me online at

www.manhoodmanual.com to buy another copy.

You can also submit your manhood stories or just

join me on the journey to manhood.

 Check out my business card too and feel

free to visit me any time on the world wide web!

Jeffrey R. Crandle
@ManhoodManual
pinterest.com/jeffreycrandle
manhoodmanual
facebook.com/jeffrey.crandle

_____ 'S MANHOOD STORY

TITLE:

_____

<u>The Cool Idea</u>

<u>The Big Problem</u>

<u>The Lesson Learned</u>

_____ 'S FORT BOX LIST

Fort Box

1.

2.

3.

4.

5.

6.

7.

8.

9.

10.

FROM THE DESK OF

_____

Dear _____:

    Hello there. There is a buzz in our community, and that buzz is about me. In case you haven't heard, I'm now a man and IT'S AWESOME! I'm going to let you in on a secret — I didn't do this all on my own. I had some help from Jeffrey R. Crandle and his book _The Manhood Manual._

    Do you want to be a man like me? Sure you do! That's why I'm giving you [my copy] [this new copy] (cross one out) of _The Manhood Manual_. Trust me dude, you need it! When you're done reading it, pass it on to someone else in need. Oh, and welcome to manhood!

Ink is low, gotta go,

_____

ABOUT THE AUTHOR AND ILLUSTRATORS

Steve Stanaszak

Steve is a partner at the law firm of Scopelitis, Garvin, Light, Hanson & Feary, P.C. in Milwaukee, Wisconsin. He focuses his practice on catastrophic injury defense and the defense of employment-related claims in the transportation industry. When he isn't working, Steve is busy trying to leave some sort of enduring impression on his two kids.

Jamie Ludovise

Jamie is an amazing freelance illustrator who lives in Orange County, California. She graduated from California State University - Long Beach, with a BFA in Animation. You can see more of her great work at www.jamieludovise.com.

18239866R00109

Made in the USA
San Bernardino, CA
20 December 2018